ENERGY

ANDREW LANGLEY

Wayland

Topics

Some of the words in this book are printed in **bold**. Their meanings are explained in the glossary on page 30.

First published in 1985 by
Wayland (Publishers) Ltd
49 Lansdowne Place, Hove
East Sussex BN3 1HF

© Copyright 1985 Wayland (Publishers) Ltd

Phototypeset by
Kalligraphics Ltd, Redhill, Surrey
Printed in Italy by
G. Canale & C.S.p.A., Turin
Bound in the UK at
The Bath Press, Avon

British Library Cataloguing in Publication Data:
Langley, Andrew
   Energy. – (Topics)
   1. Force and energy
   I. Title   II. Series
   531′.6   QC73

ISBN 0–85078–605–3

21115066M

TS

This ⌐   rned (

Contents

The Power of the Sun

Look at a blade of grass. The Sun shines down, giving it the energy to grow. Then the grass is eaten by a cow, which converts the energy from the grass into milk. The milk is put into a bottle – perhaps you drank some with your breakfast today. When you drank it, the energy passed into your body. Now the milk is being used as a fuel to keep your body warm.

Energy, as you see, can be moved from one place to another. In the process it can change into many

Energy can be moved from place to place and changed from one form to another.

Without the Sun, our food crops could not grow.

different forms. The energy keeping your body warm is simply the milk's energy in another form; the milk was produced using energy from the grass; and the grass grew because it took energy from the sunlight.

This brings us back to the Sun, which is the source of all the world's energy. Without it, our planet would be dark, cold and lifeless. It heats up the land, the water and the air, causing winds, rain and sea currents. Its light and warmth help plants to grow. The growing plants give out the **oxygen** which allows us to breathe.

In this way, the Sun is constantly recharging the Earth's store of energy. It has been doing this for thousands of millions of years. Scientists believe that it will go on pumping out energy for millions of years to come. But what is the Sun, and where does its own

The Sun is the source of all the world's energy.

power come from? Clearly it is not just an ordinary ball of fire, burning like wood or coal: if that were so it would have turned to ash long ago.

In fact, the Sun is a star and it is mostly made up of a gas called **hydrogen**. The pressure at the Sun's centre, or core, is so huge that the hydrogen is converted into **helium**. This change produces a massive amount of energy, in the form of heat. Most of the heat is lost in space, but a little of it reaches the Earth. Fortunately it is enough to allow us to live. If any more energy got through, our planet would be burned to a frazzle!

Animal Energy

Energy gives us the power to work. All living things have to work to stay alive, so they need a regular supply of energy. Even a plant works so that it can grow and make seeds for a new generation. It takes in sunlight, water and air and changes them into the sort of food it needs to do this work.

Plants do not need to move around because their energy supply comes to them. Animals have to work much harder. They cannot produce their own food from thin air, so they go out and find it. The food is taken in through their mouths and broken down by chemicals in the **digestive system**. This releases the energy to the muscles and keeps the body warm.

Even plants must work to grow and make new seeds.

Some animals, called **herbivores**, get their food directly from plants. Most of them, such as the zebra, eat grass; the giraffe browses on the tender shoots and leaves of trees; the hippopotamus grinds water plants between its huge teeth.

As long as there is plenty of sun and rain, herbivores will not go hungry. They must simply live near to the plants which they like to eat. When these run out, they move on to find fresh pastures. Many animals travel very long distances in search of fresh plants and shrubs.

But not all animals are able to digest plants. Instead these animals get their food by eating the plant-eating animals. They are still depending on plant energy, but the difference is that they wait until it has been converted into meat!

Giraffes and other herbivores get food from plants.

These meat-eaters are called **carnivores**. They have to develop special skills to help them hunt and catch other animals. Some, such as the lion or the tiger, are very strong; others, such as the cheetah, are very fast. Almost all of them are cunning and very patient to enable them to hunt and stalk their prey.

Once the food is inside them, animals can turn it into energy. But not all animals use up their energy at the same rate. A lion, for example, spends many hours asleep, saving its strength for the explosive effort of hunting. It will usually feed only once a day.

Carnivore versus herbivore: a hungry lioness chases a zebra.

The tiny shrew cannot survive unless it feeds at least every three hours.

An elephant, on the other hand, has to spend all day eating. Its massive body, which can weigh more than 6 tonnes, needs a lot of muscle to carry it about. So a full-grown elephant will need to eat at least 200 kilograms (440 lb) of grass and leaves a day, and drink 180 litres (40 gallons) of water.

It is not only the giants who have to keep stoking themselves up with energy. Small creatures lose their body heat much more quickly than big ones, so they need to feed very frequently. A shrew will die if it is kept without food for more than three hours. Birds such as finches and larks have a much higher body temperature than mammals, 44°C (111°F) instead of 37°C (98°F), and so in cold weather they have to eat almost constantly during the day.

At the other end of the scale are animals which use up energy very slowly. One of the slowest is also the laziest – the sloth. The three-toed sloth sleeps for eighteen hours a day. It lives high in the trees where there is plenty of food and no danger from

The three-toed sloth uses energy very slowly.

carnivores. It makes no noise and is virtually deaf. It has a top speed of less than 1 kilometre per hour (0.6 m.p.h.).

Human beings are **omnivores**, which means we can eat both plants and meat. We need and produce energy in just the same way as other animals, but with one vital difference. We have learned to harness the muscle power of the stronger creatures around us. For centuries, oxen have pulled ploughs, and horses have carried people overland.

Human beings use stronger animals to help us carry heavy loads.

Fuel from the Ground

So far the types of energy we have looked at have been 'instant' fuels. Plants get energy straight from the Sun, and we get ours straight from the food we eat. But energy can also be stored away for long periods without losing any of its power. By discovering and using these stores of energy, humans have been able to change the world in many startling ways.

The first and greatest discovery was how to make fire. By striking a **flint**, or rubbing two sticks

Fire changes the energy stored in tree wood into heat and light.

Steam power was used to drive this early locomotive.

together, people found that they could set light to wood. The trees contained stored energy from the Sun, and fire converted that into heat and light. With fire people could cook, keep warm and melt metal so that it could be shaped into tools.

The next step was to convert the heat into yet another kind of energy – steam. If water is boiled, it turns into steam. If that steam is put into a confined place and then cooled, it will form a **vacuum**. The pull of the vacuum can be used to move a **piston**, which in turn can be used to rotate a wheel.

The invention of the steam engine in the eighteenth century was the beginning of the age known as the Industrial Revolution. Soon steam power was driving ships and railway locomotives.

Steam also helped drive machines to spin cotton, weave cloth and thresh wheat.

Coal is an important source of energy. This black rock is actually formed from prehistoric plants which have decayed and compressed over millions of years. By burning it, we are obtaining energy from very ancient sunlight indeed. Coal's great value is that it gives out much more heat than wood does.

Coal and steam power are still widely used today, though not often for transport or for driving machines. But by adding yet another link to the energy chain, coal and steam power can now produce electricity.

A huge opencast coal mine and, in the background, a power station.

In some power stations, powdered coal is burned in a furnace. Others use oil instead. The enormous heat in the furnace turns water into steam, which drives the blades of a **turbine**. The turbine rotates heavy coils of wire between the two poles of a giant magnet. This is a generator, which gives out a charge of electricity.

Here you can see how energy can be changed into a great variety of forms. From the sunlight it passes through plants, coal, steam and the generator to become an entirely different kind of power.

In this power station, the energy contained in coal is changed into electrical energy.

The electricity in our homes may come from coal, which was formed from decayed prehistoric plants.

Electricity can then be turned back into mechanical energy and used to drive machines in factories or in our homes. It can be turned back into heat through electric fires. Or it can be turned back into light through the filament of a light bulb.

There is a lot of coal left in the world. But it is hard to dig up and heavy to move. It has to be broken up before it will burn well. Oil is a much easier fuel to deal with because it is a liquid. When a hole is drilled to an underground oil well, the oil gushes out. From the oil field it is moved through pipes to the **refinery**.

An oil refinery in the Netherlands.

Like coal, oil is a **fossil fuel**. It was formed millions of years ago from the decaying remains of tiny plants and animals. When it is refined, it can be used as fuel for cars, aircraft and power stations.

Wherever there is oil underground, natural gas will be found too. It is piped to towns and cities and burned in our homes for cooking and heating.

All our supplies of coal, oil and gas are limited. One day they will be used up, so it is important to look for other sources of energy.

Splitting the Atom

Everything on Earth is made up of atoms, all of
them far too small to see. Yet these tiny blocks of
matter contain a massive amount of energy. When
that energy is released, it is many times more
powerful than coal, oil or gas.

At the heart of an atom is the **nucleus**, made up of
particles called **protons** and **neutrons**. But not all
atoms are the same: some have more protons than
others. Hydrogen, for example, has only one proton
in its nucleus; aluminium has 13; and at the far end

This atom has 6 protons and 6 neutrons in its nucleus.

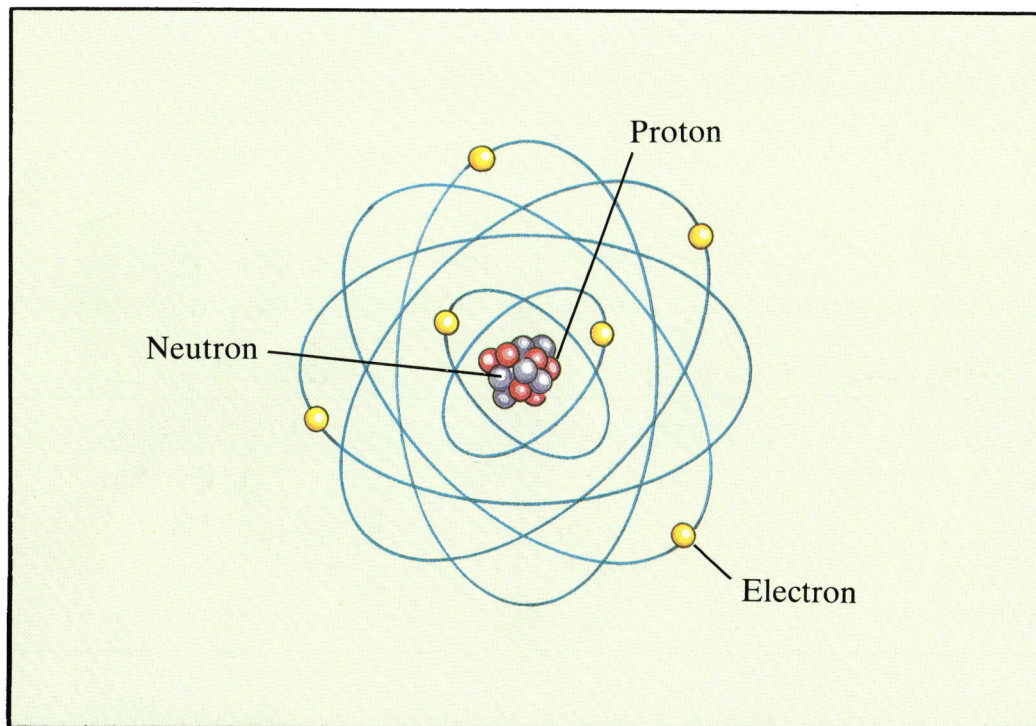

of the scale is a metal called uranium, with 92.

With so many protons jostling together, it is not surprising that uranium gives out energy all the time. This energy is called **radiation**. If the uranium is left alone, the radiation will continue at a steady rate for many centuries.

Scientists have found that they can 'split' uranium nuclei by firing neutrons at them. When a neutron, travelling at incredible speed, smashes into a uranium nucleus the nucleus is split in two. More neutrons are also produced, and these shoot off and split the nuclei of nearby uranium atoms.

Nuclear fission: if a neutron is fired at a uranium nucleus, it splits the nucleus in two. Other neutrons are released and may split other uranium nuclei, and so on. Fission produces a lot of heat.

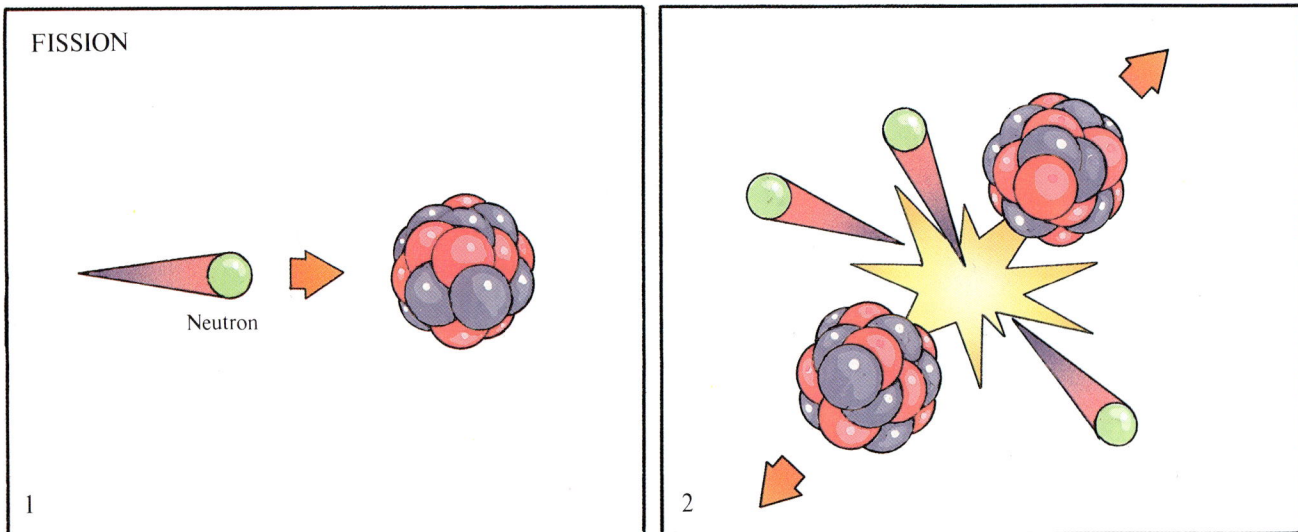

FISSION

Neutron

1

2

Inside a nuclear power station.

The splitting (**nuclear fission**) causes heat to be given out. This is how we produce nuclear energy.

Nuclear energy can be used in horrible ways, in bombs which can destroy thousands of people. But it can also be used in a good way, to produce electricity. Throughout the world there are now more than 500 power stations run on nuclear energy.

The advantage of nuclear power is that it uses very little fuel. One tonne of uranium can produce as much energy as a million tonnes of coal. The first nuclear submarine, the *Nautilus*, travelled twice around the world using a piece of fuel the size of a tennis ball.

The nuclear submarine Nautilus.

The Energy of the Future

Today, more than ever before, we depend on the stored energy of fossil fuels. Coal, oil and gas give us heat and electricity. From oil we make petrol to power our cars. We also use oil to make plastics, which have a thousand uses. Natural gas is turned into fertilizer which helps our food crops to grow.

But these fuels will not last for ever. The world burns up a million barrels of oil every hour, and by the end of this century supplies may be running low.

These plastic items are all made from oil.

This is an experimental nuclear fusion reactor.

There is still plenty of coal to mine, but even this will run out one day.

What will replace them? Scientists are working hard to find an answer. The most obvious one is nuclear power, which can produce a lot of heat from a small amount of fuel. Sadly, however, it has one major drawback: the splitting of the uranium nucleus causes many dangerous new atoms to be formed. No one has yet found a way of making this nuclear waste safe, so it has to be buried deep in the Earth.

There is, however, a harmless kind of nuclear energy. For years, scientists have dreamed of joining nuclei together to make energy, instead of splitting them up. This, after all, is the way that the Sun makes its energy. The process (called **nuclear fusion**) leaves no dangerous waste, and needs only hydrogen as a fuel. Scientists are working on nuclear fusion, but as yet they have not solved all the problems involved.

In the meantime, we can make better use of the Sun itself. Mirrors can be used to reflect sunlight into a furnace, and this produces enough heat to turn water into steam. This steam can be used to make electric power.

In this solar power station, 1,800 mirrors reflect the sunlight into a furnace.

Solar cells on a telecommunications satellite.

Electricity can also be made directly from the Sun's rays. When they fall on special plates, called **solar cells**, an electric charge is produced. Space ships and satellites use the Sun's energy in this way.

Many other natural forces are being put to use today. Water, for instance, always runs downhill. If a river is blocked by a dam, the water quickly builds up. When it is released in a controlled flow, it can be made to turn a turbine to produce electricity. **Hydro-electric** dams, using water to produce electricity, have been built all over the world.

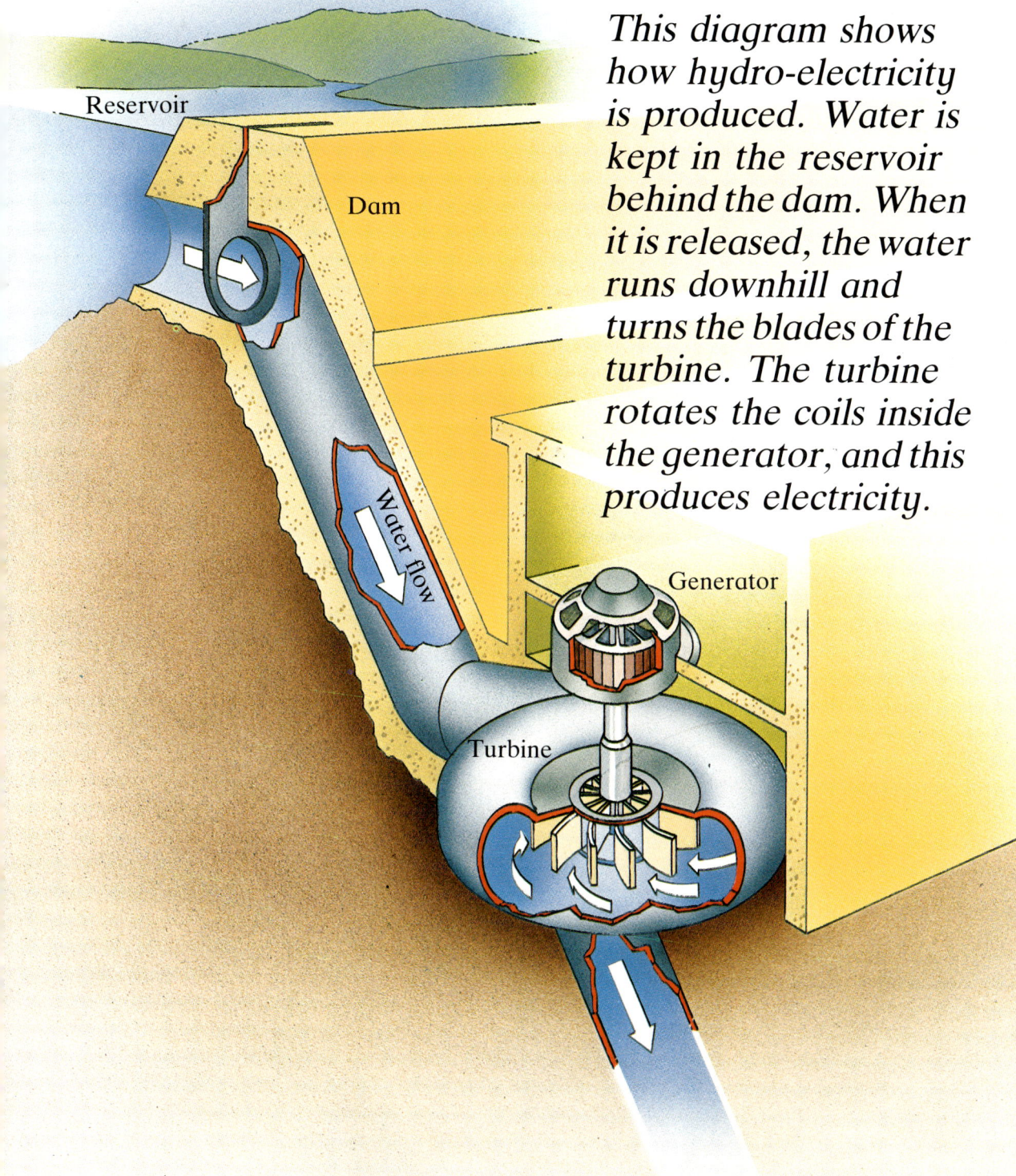

Reservoir

Dam

Water flow

Generator

Turbine

This diagram shows how hydro-electricity is produced. Water is kept in the reservoir behind the dam. When it is released, the water runs downhill and turns the blades of the turbine. The turbine rotates the coils inside the generator, and this produces electricity.

Water in the oceans is never still. Scientists are exploring ways of generating electricity from the movement of the waves and tides. One idea is to float a series of boxes which will nod up and down with the waves, and so move a turbine and make electricity.

The wind can also be used to make electricity by turning the sails of a windmill. But it is unreliable – one day there may be no wind, and the next a howling gale! Perhaps a more valuable use of wind

A row of modern windmills, or 'aerogenerators'.

A geyser in New Zealand; the heat of the Earth may be a valuable source of energy for the future.

power is to blow cargo ships along. New ships and sails are now being designed which may one day take over from oil-driven vessels.

Lastly, there is the heat of the Earth itself. At its centre it is so hot that the rock melts and boils. In some places, hot springs of water bubble to the surface, bringing ready-made steam for power stations.

None of these forms of power has yet given us the answer to our energy problems. The best we can do is make sure that we don't squander what we have got. By making machines which use less fuel, and by re-using waste products, we can make our resources last much longer.

Glossary

Carnivore An animal that eats meat.

Digestive system The way food goes through the body and is broken down to release energy.

Flint A very hard rock that produces a spark when struck.

Fossil fuel A fuel such as coal or oil which was formed by the decaying of ancient plants and animals.

Helium A very light gas sometimes used to fill airships and balloons.

Herbivore An animal that eats plants.

Hydro-electric power Electricity generated by using the power of running water.

Hydrogen Colourless, odourless, tasteless gas. Combined with oxygen, it forms water.

Neutron One of the types of particle found in the nucleus of an atom.

Nuclear fission The splitting of atomic nuclei to produce energy.

Nuclear fusion The joining of atomic nuclei together to produce energy.

Nucleus The core of an atom. The plural of nucleus is nuclei.

Omnivore An animal that eats both plants and animals.

Oxygen An odourless, invisible gas contained in the air we breathe. Without it there would be no life on Earth.

Piston A cylinder which fits into a slightly larger hollow block and moves up and down under pressure.

Proton One of the types of particle found in the nucleus of an atom.

Radiation The energy given out by a radioactive material such as uranium.

Refinery A place where oil is purified and split up into different products such as diesel oil, petrol and gas.

Solar cell A device that turns the Sun's energy into electricity.

Turbine A machine which uses moving steam, air, or water to turn a generator to make electricity.

Vacuum A space in which there are no atoms; or a space containing air or another gas at very low pressure.

Books to Read

Asimov's Guide to Science by Isaac Asimov (Penguin, 1975)
Focus on Alternative Energy by Paul McClory (Wayland, 1985)
Focus on Nuclear Fuel by Vivienne Driscoll (Wayland, 1985)
Energy: The Fuel of Life by the Editors of the Encyclopedia Britannica (Bantam, 1979)
Energy by Desmond Boyle (Macdonald Educational, 1980)
The Gas in Your Home by Angela and Derek Lucas (Wayland, 1982)
How We Found Out About Energy by Isaac Asimov (Longman, 1982)
Looking at Energy by Don Radford (Batsford, 1984)

Picture Acknowledgements

The illustrations in this book were supplied by: British Nuclear Fuels Ltd 21; Bruce Coleman 6 (Stepen J. Krasemann), 8 (Jen and Des Bartlett), 9 (Gunter Ziesler), 10 (Jane Burton), 11 (Michael Fogden); Camerapix Hutchison Library 13 (W. Jesco von Puttkamer); Central Electricity Generating Board 16; NHPA 7 (Jerg Kroener); PHOTRI 22; Picturepoint 2; Shell 18, 23; Southern California Edison Co 25, 28; Telefocus 26; Malcolm S. Walker 4, 17, 19, 20, 27; Wayland Picture Library 14, 15; ZEFA 12, 19.

Index